Fans Love Reading *Choose Your Own Adventure*®!

"I like all the different endings. Some are funny and some are weird, but they are all interesting."

Ellie Smart, Age 7

"I like CYOA because it's like you're writing your own book!"

Kyle Smart, Age 5

"We have had these books in our library ever since their first publishing. They have never gone out of demand."

Jean Closz,
Blount County Public Library, Tennessee

CHOOSE YOUR OWN ADVENTURE®

OWL TREE

BY R. A. MONTGOMERY

A DRAGONLARK BOOK

Illustrated by: Gabhor Uotomo
Book design: Stacey Boyd, Big Eyedea Visual Design
For information regarding permission, write to:

CHOOSECO
P.O. Box 46
Waitsfield, Vermont 05673
www.cyoa.com

A DRAGONLARK BOOK
ISBN: 1-933390-80-8
EAN: 978-1-933390-80-2

Published simultaneously in the United States and Canada

Printed in the United States of America.

0 9 8 7 6 5 4 3 2 1

For Ramsey

A DRAGONLARK BOOK

READ THIS FIRST!!!

WATCH OUT!
THIS BOOK IS DIFFERENT
than every book you've ever read.

Don't believe me?

Have you ever read a book that was about YOU?

This book is!

YOU get to choose what happens next
—and even how the story will end.

DON'T READ THIS BOOK FROM
THE FIRST PAGE TO THE LAST.

Read until you reach a choice.
Turn to the page of the choice you like best.
If you don't like the end you reach, just start over!

The day you discovered the owl tree was magical. You were hiking in the forest near your house when you stumbled into a large clearing. In the center of it stood a maple tree. Its trunk was so thick that four kids linking hands would barely circle it!

As you stood under the tree looking up, you were surprised by several questions.

"Whooo?"

"Whoooo?"

"Whooooo?"

"It's me," you replied, wondering who was asking, "who?"

Then a bunch of owls poked their heads out of the tree. You spent the day there and learned many of the owls' secrets.

Turn to the next page.

Today your best friend, Sally, is coming to the owl tree with you. It's a sunny Saturday—a perfect day for a hike in the woods. You lace up your hiking boots, strap on your backpack, and head for the corner of your street where Sally is waiting.

When the two of you reach the clearing, you stand still. Softly you call, "Whooo? Whooo?" Minutes later some owls pop out of the tree.

"What happens now?" asks Sally.

"We can follow an owl to a magic kingdom," you say. "But we'll have to wait until one leaves."

"What's the other choice?" she asks.

"We can ask the owls some questions. They're very wise."

"You decide," Sally answers. "You've been here before."

If you wait and follow an owl to a magic kingdom, turn to page 4.

If you decide to ask the owls questions, turn to page 8.

You and Sally settle down to wait. The forest floor is soft and the day is warm. The owls watch you. They swivel their heads back and forth and blink their huge eyes.

Suddenly a barn owl leaves with a flap of wings.

"One's leaving," you shout. "Let's go."

Turn to the next page.

You and Sally take off after the owl. The forest is thick with trees and plants. The owl soars above them, dipping in and out of view. As you run, you trip over roots and stumble over bushes.

Suddenly you come to a wide river. You look up, but the owl is gone! To the right of the river is a well-used trail. On your left stands a high stone wall. It looks old and crumbly.

"Drat!" you say to Sally. "Which way should we go?"

If you decide to follow the trail, turn to page 11.

If you decide to climb over the wall, turn to page 14.

If you decide to cross the river, turn to page 21.

8

You step close to the owl tree and ask in your most polite voice, "Oh, owls, most wise owls, what will I be when I grow up?"

A small saw-whet owl leans forward and speaks in a whisper. "If you are prepared to carry out my every command, then I will reveal your future."

"Forget it, owl," Sally says. "I have enough commands to obey. My big brother bosses me around all the time!"

You don't know what to do. Who knows what this owl will command? Maybe you can get one of the other owls to answer your question.

If you ask the saw-whet owl what he wants you to do, turn to page 12.

If you ask a different owl about your future, turn to page 16.

"I see something moving over there," you say, pointing down the trail. "Let's go that way."

You and Sally follow the trail for awhile. Along the way you spot a strange-looking bush with two bright yellow flowers. As you step toward it there's a flash of wings. Two bright yellow eyes—not flowers—blink at you. It's the owl!

With a loud hoot he flies off above the trail.

You and Sally follow as best you can on the ground.

Finally the owl makes a left by an oak tree, and you round the corner after him. You don't see the owl anywhere, but hanging from a oak tree is a plump leather sack.

If you decide to look in the sack, turn to page 33.

If you decide to keep looking for the owl, turn to page 40.

12

"What would you like me to do?" you ask the saw-whet owl.

"Bring me fresh raspberries from the bushes of Illnoor," the saw-whet owl replies, blinking his eyes.

"What's Illnoor?" you ask.

"It's the home of the Great Zoonies. They are large and very mean creatures. They guard the raspberry bushes."

"That sounds dangerous!" Sally snaps. Then she turns to you. "I'm not going anywhere. Are you going to Illnoor?"

If you travel alone to Illnoor, turn to page 19.

If you tell the owl you won't go, turn to page 25.

You and Sally each grab hold of a sturdy stone in the wall to pull yourselves up. You manage to climb about three feet from the bottom. But when you look up, you see that the top of the wall isn't getting any closer. Then it hits you: as you climb it, this old stone wall is growing!

"I don't think we're getting anywhere," Sally shouts. "What do you think we should do?"

If you say, "Let's jump off this wall," turn to page 24.

If you say, "Let's keep trying to climb this old wall," turn to page 28.

16

You look up at a horned owl. "Oh, horned owl, you look wiser than the little saw-whet owl. Can you tell me what I'll be when I grow up?"

The horned owl clears his throat. He's about to answer you when the saw-whet owl speaks up.

"Just wait one minute, my friend! I'm just as wise—or wiser! I'll prove it, too. Ask me another question."

You can't decide. Should you ask the horned owl what you will be when you grow up, or ask both of them a new question?

If you ask the horned owl the same question, turn to page 20.

If you ask both owls a new question, turn to page 23.

It doesn't take long to get to Illnoor. From a distance you can see the Great Zoonies and they look harmless. They're furry creatures shaped like caterpillars—only bigger.

Turn to page 42.

"What am I going to be when I grow up?" you ask for the second time. You wait patiently while the owl stretches to his full height. He rearranges his feathers. He blinks his eyes. Finally he speaks.

"That's a difficult question. A very difficult question. You could be a teacher or a writer or a doctor or a lawyer or an artist or a builder or anything you want to be. You'll have to wait and find out."

The saw-whet owl hoots good-bye as he and the other owls duck back into the owl tree. As you and Sally hike home through the forest, you think about the owl's answer. You wish he told you more about your future, but you know he's right—what happens is up to you!

The End

"I thought I saw him on the other side of the river. Let's try to cross it," you say.

You look for a way to get to the other side. Luckily, there's an old wooden boat pulled up on the bank. The oars are still in it.

"Let's borrow the boat," you say.

"Maybe we shouldn't. It's not ours," Sally says.

Turn to the next page.

"This boat hasn't been used in a long time. Look at all the leaves in the bottom," you reply. "We can return it after we find the owl."

The two of you push the boat into the river and jump aboard. You begin to row across. But the river is flowing very fast and the boat gets caught in its swift current.

"Help, Sally! I can't control the boat!" you yell.

Turn to page 27.

You decide to ask the owl a new question. You huddle with Sally. Finally you speak up.

"Oh wise and great owls, what will happen to the world?"

There is silence. You can hear yourself breathe and the tree's leaves gently rubbing together.

Turn to page 37.

Just as you and Sally are about to drop to the ground, the barn owl lands on top of the wall. He peers down at you.

"Too late, too late," he says. "You should have tried to climb to the top of the wall. I would have shown you the Castle of Remembrance where dreams stay alive. We would have visited the Hall of Flowers where spring and summer never end. Oh well, maybe we'll visit another day."

Then the owl disappears and the stone wall shrinks. To the west you see the sun sinking behind the trees. It's too late today for any more exploring, but you'll go back to the owl tree another day!

The End

When you refuse to go to Illnoor, the saw-whet owl stares hard at you. He looks mad, but you don't care. You're not about to change your mind!

Finally the owl winks at you and Sally. Then he says, "I was just testing you. You've responded wisely to my request. So, now I'll tell you what the future holds. Ready?"

You yell, "Ready!" The owl shifts his feathers.

Turn to page 43.

Just then the barn owl flies overhead.

"Took on a bit too much today, I see," he says in a squeaky voice.

"He talks!" Sally shouts, so surprised that she almost falls over the side of the boat.

"Please help us, owl," you beg. "This boat is out of control!"

"Go with the current and aim for shore when you get close to the bank of the river," the owl replies wisely. "You'll be safe."

Your boat bounces in the rough water while you watch the owl fly away. Finally the river bends, and you use the oars to steer the boat toward the bank. It bumps up on a sandy beach.

"I don't know about you, Sally," you say as you climb out of the boat, "but I think home will look like a magic kingdom after this boat ride!"

The End

You and Sally back away from the wall and begin to count.

"One...two...three...GO!"

And suddenly you're both sitting on top of it—almost as if you flew!

When you look down over the wall, you see a castle surrounded by an old-fashioned town. Tiny people are running around busily. Some are adding bricks to a fort outside the castle. Others are hooking up horses to carts.

"It's the Kingdom of Gollop," says a calm voice beside you.

Turn to the next page.

The barn owl is sitting on the wall next to you!

"It's a shame you can't visit Gollop right now," the owl continues. "The Gollops are getting ready to battle the Evil Fotons."

But before you ask the owl more about Gollop and the Evil Fotons, the wall shrinks to its normal size and the kingdom disappears.

The owl is gone.

Turn to page 39.

You shimmy up the trunk of the oak tree and crawl along a thin brown branch. As you reach for the sack you hear the branch bend.

"Watch out!" Sally cries.

Crack! Wham! Thud!

The sack, branch, and you fall to the ground!

You're not hurt, but the sack is. A strange light spills from the tear and spreads on the ground like a puddle of water.

Turn to the next page.

"Sallllllllly. Sallllllllyyyy!" you say in a frightened whisper. She is hiding behind you.

"What is that stuff?" she asks.

At that very moment the light gathers together, rises off the ground, and swirls into a cloudy shape. Slowly the figure of the creature—half owl, half stag—appears.

"I am the spirit of this forest. I rule the birds, the wind, the sky, the sunlight, the rain, and all the animals. I will grant you one wish. What will it be?" The creature waits for you to answer.

What is your wish?

You decide.

The End

The saw-whet owl looks nervous. The great horned owl rolls his round eyes.

"The world will survive. There will be hard times and even dangerous times, but the world will survive. You must help it, though."

How will you help?

The End

"I guess we're not going to see a magic kingdom today," you say to Sally as you jump down from the wall. "Let's head back to the owl tree and see if we can get the owls to answer some questions."

When you get back to the tree several owls are sitting in its branches.

Turn to page 8.

You turn toward the forest—the owl may have gone that way. But Sally stays right where she is. "I want to look in the sack," she says. "I'll catch up with you later."

You follow a muddy trail for a short while. But as you hike deeper into the woods, moss and large tree roots sprawl over the path. And the trees and bushes become thicker, blocking out the sun. Your heart races a little—it's pretty dark here!

You hike about half a mile, but there's still no sign of the owl. You lean against a tree and close your eyes. You rest for a few minutes. But suddenly you hear some leaves rustle, and then another noise—like footsteps.

Who's coming? you wonder nervously. It may be Sally catching up to you. On the other hand it could be something dangerous—like a bear looking for dinner!

If you break into a run, turn to page 44.

If you think it's Sally and stay where you are, turn to page 45.

When you enter Illnoor, the Great Zoonies welcome you and invite you to a feast of raspberries. After you stuff yourself with the juicy berries, you rest in the warm sun. You explain to the Great Zoonies why you've come. They tell you that the saw-whet owl always tries to steal the raspberries. "If only he'd ask," one says with a sigh. "We'd give him all the berries he wanted."

You decide to stay with the Great Zoonies. From time to time you miss Sally and your family. And you wonder if the saw-whet owl is still waiting for you. But you no longer need the owl's wisdom. Now you know that your future will be a happy life in Illnoor!

The End

Suddenly a bigger saw-whet owl swoops out of the owl tree.

"Okay, Sammy. That's enough for today," she says. "Stop teasing those humans."

The small saw-whet owl disappears into a hole in the owl tree. Then the larger one looks at you and Sally and says, "Owls are very wise, but even we can't tell the future!"

The End

You run as fast as you can. You are out of breath when you get back to the oak tree. Sally is crawling along one of its branches.

"Hello!" she cries. "You're as white as a ghost. Did the owl scare you?"

"I thought you might need some help back here," you say quickly. There's no need to explain that you just ran away from a noise!

Sally reaches for the sack. But before she can grab it, it shakes loose from the branch. Suddenly it has wings…the sack is a horned owl!

The owl circles overhead and then rests on a branch. "Why have you entered my forest?" he demands.

Turn to
page 47.

You stand up straight against the tree and wait for whoever, or whatever, is coming. You hope it's Sally!

The footsteps sound closer and closer. Finally a clump of bushes parts, and Sally steps through it! Her face is red with excitement.

"Boy am I glad to see you," you say.

"Never mind that," she says. "Look what I found in the sack." She puts something heavy into your hand.

Turn to the next page.

You look at what Sally has given you. It's a long gold bar and carved into it are the words:

ADMIT 2 TO THE KINGDOM OF GOLLOP.

"The Kingdom of Gollop," you say. "That's a secret kingdom. One of the owls told me about it when I found the owl tree."

Then you look up. The barn owl is circling over your heads. "Come on, owl!" you shout. "Lead the way to Gollop!"

The End

Quickly you step forward. "We're sorry, Mr. Owl—if you are a mister owl. We didn't mean to trespass. We didn't hurt anything, honest."

"Harrumph! A likely story," he responds. "Well, get going. This is my forest, and I say out. Now!"

"Let's go home," you say to Sally. "Whooo knows what this mean old owl will do!"

The End

Watch for these titles coming up in the

CHOOSE YOUR OWN ADVENTURE®

Dragonlarks® series for Beginning Readers

ALWAYS PICKED LAST
YOUR VERY OWN ROBOT GOES CUCKOO-BANANAS
RETURN TO HAUNTED HOUSE
THE OWL TREE
THE LAKE MONSTER MYSTERY
YOUR VERY OWN ROBOT
THE HAUNTED HOUSE
YOUR PURRR-FECT BIRTHDAY
SAND CASTLE
GHOST ISLAND
INDIAN TRAIL
CARAVAN

 Purchase online at www.cyoa.com or ask your local bookseller

CREDITS

Illustrator: Gabhor Uotomo was born in Indonesia. He moved to California to pursue his passion in art. He received his degree from Academy of Art University in San Francisco in spring 2003. Since graduation, he's worked as a freelance illustrator and has illustrated a number of children's books. Gabhor lives with his wife, Dina, and his twin girls in San Francisco Bay Area.

ABOUT THE AUTHOR

R. A. Montgomery has hiked in the Himalayas, climbed mountains in Europe, scuba-dived in Central America, and worked in Africa. He lives in France in the winter, travels frequently to Asia, and calls Vermont home. Montgomery graduated from Williams College and attended graduate school at Yale University and NYU. His interests include macroeconomics, geo-politics, mythology, history, mystery novels, and music. He has two grown sons, a daughter-in-law, and two granddaughters. His wife, Shannon Gilligan, is an author and noted interactive game designer. Montgomery feels that the new generation of people under 15 is the most important asset in our world.

**For games, activities and other fun stuff,
or to write to R. A. Montgomery,
visit us online at www.cyoa.com**